HOW DO YOU HUG A PORCUPINE?

By
Laurie Isop

Illustrated by
Gwen Millward

Simon & Schuster Books for Young Readers
NEW YORK LONDON TORONTO SYDNEY

To my father, Ron Austin, who always gave the very best hugs
—L. I.

To Myfanwy, with love
—G. M.

ACKNOWLEDGMENTS
Thank you to Paul, Austin, and Erik for tolerating my prickly
side, and to my dear family and friends—Debbie, Joyce, Cheryl,
Annette, Anh-Thu, Ping, Sandi, Maria, Suresh, Richard, Mark,
and Gregg—for believing in me.
—L. I.

SIMON & SCHUSTER BOOKS FOR YOUNG READERS • An imprint of Simon & Schuster
Children's Publishing Division • 1230 Avenue of the Americas, New York, New York 10020
• Text copyright © 2011 by Laurie Isop • Illustrations copyright © 2011 by Gwen Millward •
All rights reserved, including the right of reproduction in whole or in part in any form. SIMON
& SCHUSTER BOOKS FOR YOUNG READERS is a trademark of Simon & Schuster, Inc. • Book design by
Chloë Foglia • The text for this book is set in Barcelona. • The illustrations for this book were
rendered in lead-based pencil, watercolor paint, and acrylic ink on Daler-Rowney heavyweight
paper. Inspiration was provided by Gwen's pet rabbit and muse, Saskia (a.k.a. Sassy the bun).
Manufactured in Mexico
ISBN 978-1-4424-1291-0

Can you hug a horse?
Of course!

A cow?
With arms around her neck,
that's how.

A dog or cat is not so hard.

Just hug them in your own backyard.

Hugging bunnies is just divine.

But how do you hug a porcupine?

Can you hug some billy goats?
Entice them with a bag of oats!

And surely you can hug a pig;
just spread your arms out
E X T R A big.

With baby chicks
be sweet, be kind.

But how do you hug

a porcupine?

This prickly fellow won't be easy.
(My stomach's feeling kind of queasy!)

He wears a coat of thorny quills.
To hug this one will take some skills!

A hedgehog is
a little prickly.

An ostrich is
a little tickly.

A chimpanzee
will hug you back.

I've never tried
to hug a yak.

A giraffe requires quite a climb.

But how do you hug a porcupine?

An elephant?
Please hug his trunk.

I wouldn't want to hug a skunk!

A kangaroo?
Just hop this way!

Don't let the dolphins
slip away!

A panda probably
wouldn't mind.

But how do you hug a porcupine?

You must go slowly; never hurry.

Porcupines aren't soft and furry.

His quills defend him from his foes,

but I'm his friend, he surely knows.

At last! Hooray! It's finally time!

THIS is how you hug a porcupine:

CAREFULLY!